The Trip to Grandma's

Written by Cass Hollander

Illustrated by Stan Tusan

SCHOLASTIC INC.

New York   Toronto   London   Auckland   Sydney

Copyright © 1994 by Scholastic Inc.
All rights reserved. Published by Scholastic Inc.
Printed in the U.S.A.
ISBN 0-590-27600-X

4 5 6 7 8 9 10   08   00 99 98 97 96

"Let's go to Grandma's," Mom said.

3

So we all got into the car.

Along the way, we saw some horses.
"Let's stop and pet the horses,"
said my brother Hank.

Mom stopped the car and we all jumped out.
We played with the horses for a while.

"Let's get going now," said Mom.
So we all got into the car.

Along the way, we saw a stream.
"Let's go for a little swim," said my sister Amy Lee.

8

Mom stopped the car and we all jumped out.
We went for a nice little swim.

"We really should get going now," said Mom.
So we all got back into the car.

Along the way, we saw some apple trees.
"Let's stop and pick apples," I said.

Mom stopped the car and we all jumped out.
We picked apples for a while.

"We really should get going now," said Mom.
So we all got back into the car.

We finally got to Grandma's house.

We hugged her hello and
we gave her some apples.

"We really should get going now," said Mom.
Then we all got back into the car.